Bee is telling Phonic about Inky. Inky is not feeling well and Bee has sent her to bed.

Bee peeps into the bedroom and sees Inky asleep. She looks again. Inky has big red spots.

Ding dong! Here is Snake. He has come to visit Inky.

Bee looks at Snake and then at Snake's spots, and will not let him in.

"You have given Inky your spots!" Bee tells Snake. "She is not feeling well at all."

"Er, Bee," interrupts Phonic, "I think you had better look in the mirror."

"I have got spots too!" Bee cries.

Snake and Phonic send Bee to bed as well. Then Snake brings hot drinks for Inky and Bee.

Next morning, Doctor West visits the house to see Inky and Bee.

Snake tells Doctor West about the spots, and that Bee thinks she and Inky got them from him.

Doctor West looks at Inky and Bee, and then at Snake. They *all* have spots.

Snake has spots on his spots!

“I am glad *I* cannot get spots,” thinks Phonic.

Doctor West tells Bee and Inky that they did not get the spots from Snake, and that they will soon be better.

Inky's and Bee's spots will all vanish, but Snake will have some spots forever.